YER SAY BOO!

by
ROBIN PULVER

illustrated by
DEB LUCKE

Holiday House / *New York*

For the heroic fire drill experts
at Fairport Road: David, Tim, Matthew,
Dan, Bryan, and Andy.
And for the heroic
Heritage Christian
Services staff.
I love you all!
— R. P.

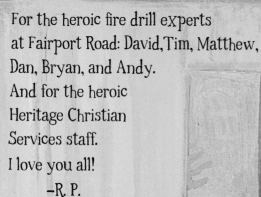

Library of Congress Cataloging-in-Publication Data
Pulver, Robin.
Never say boo! / by Robin Pulver ; illustrated by Deb Lucke. – 1st ed.
p. cm.
Summary: When Gordon, a ghost, moves to a new school, everyone is afraid
of him until they learn that he is not as scary as they thought he was.
ISBN 978-0-8234-2110-7 (hardcover)
[1. Ghosts–Fiction. 2. Schools–Fiction.] I. Lucke, Deb, ill. II. Title.
PZ7.P97325Ne 2009
[E]–dc21
2008022609

"Being the new kid is a bummer," muttered Gordon, as he drifted through the halls of Booniesville Elementary School.

At his old school in Ghost Town, everybody was a ghost. But at Booniesville, Gordon was the only one.

Finally Gordon found his classroom and went inside.

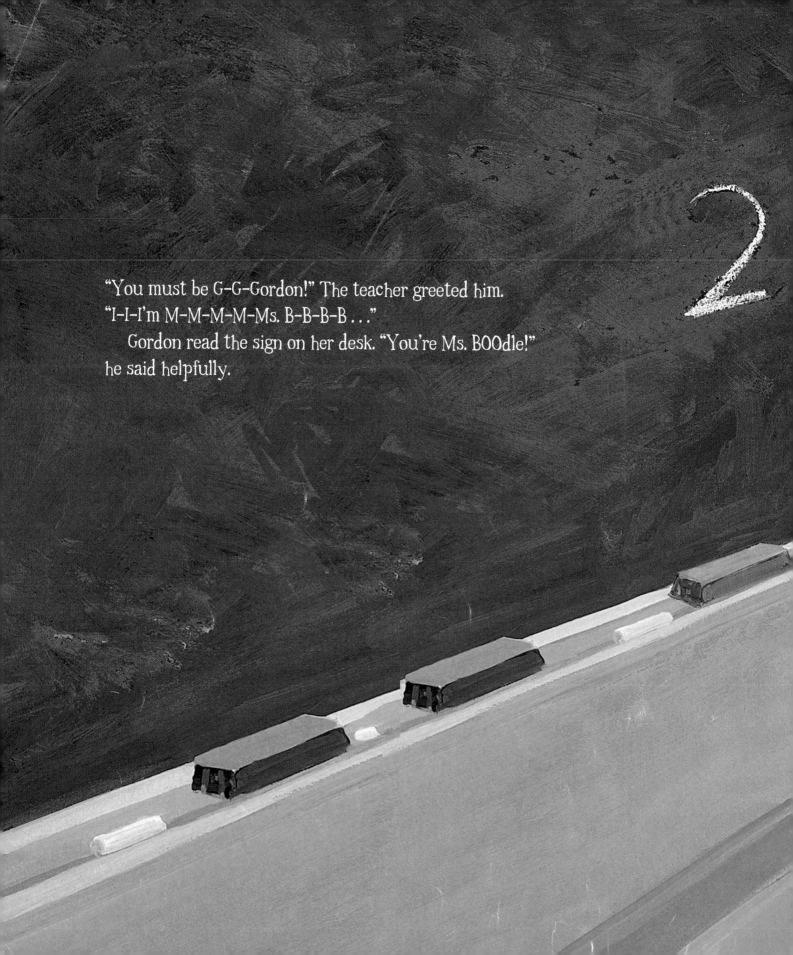

"You must be G–G–Gordon!" The teacher greeted him.
"I–I–I'm M–M–M–M–Ms. B–B–B–B . . ."

Gordon read the sign on her desk. "You're Ms. BOOdle!"
he said helpfully.

Ms. Boodle fainted.
"EEEEEEEEEK!" went
the kids in the room.
SCREEEEEEECH! went
their chairs.

Gordon's new teacher lay
on the floor, passed out cold.
Otherwise, the classroom was
as deserted as a graveyard
without ghosts.

"Bummer," muttered Gordon.
When Ms. Boodle came to,
she gathered the children back
into the room.

"C-C-Class," sputtered Ms. Boodle. "This is Gordon. His f-f-family moved into the old abandoned house r-r-right across the street from s-s-school!"

Ms. Boodle smiled shakily. "Gordon, when new students join our class, we invite them to share a special talent with us. Do you have a talent to share?"

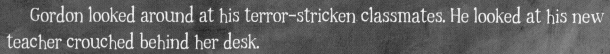

Gordon looked around at his terror-stricken classmates. He looked at his new teacher crouched behind her desk.

Gordon had won the prize for the scariest *BOO!* at his old school in Ghost Town. Sadly, Gordon realized that his prize-winning, blood-curdling, hair-raising *BOO!* would not win him a single new friend here.

"No," said Gordon. "I don't have a talent to share."
"Very well, G-Gordon," said Ms. Boodle. "Perhaps you need t-t-time to get used to us. P-Please take the empty seat between Lisa and J-Jason."

Lisa looked so scared
her eyes spun in their sockets.
Gordon rolled his eyes
back at her.
Lisa shrieked and ran into
the girls' bathroom.

"You're not supposed to roll your eyes at girls," Jason said.

"You're not?" asked Gordon. "How do *you* make friends with girls?"

"I hide and then jump out at them and say BOO!" said Jason.

Ms. Boodle announced, "All of today's vocabulary words have the same double vowel. First, I am thinking of an object from Australia that can be thrown so that it returns to the thrower. Who knows what it is?"

Gordon knew the answer, but he knew he shouldn't say it.

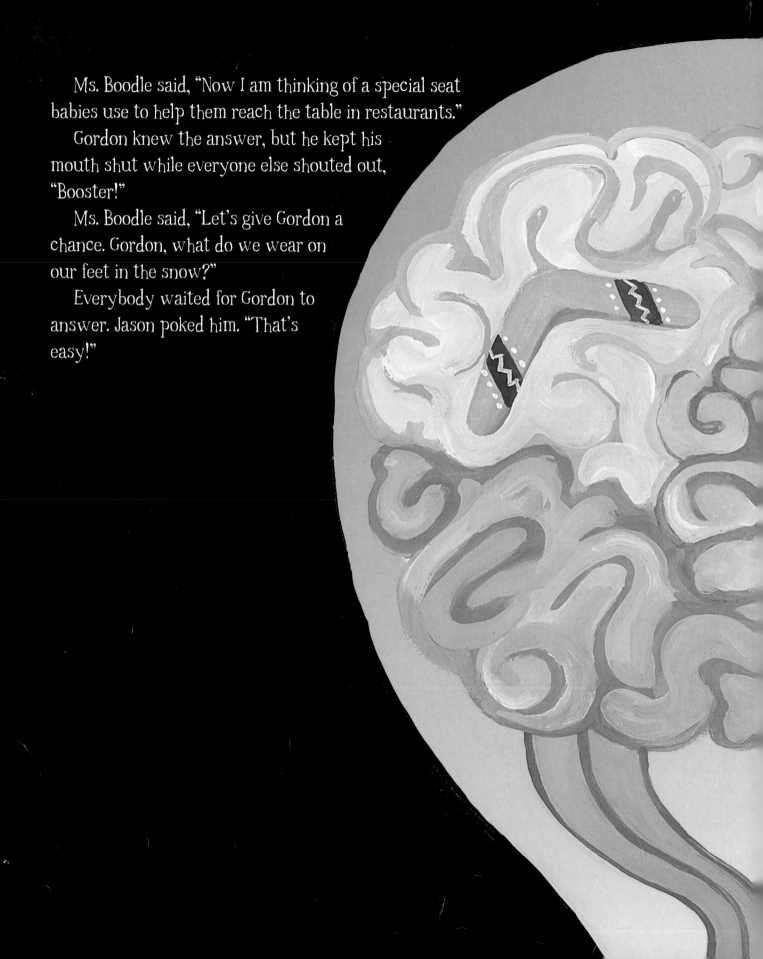

Ms. Boodle said, "Now I am thinking of a special seat babies use to help them reach the table in restaurants."

Gordon knew the answer, but he kept his mouth shut while everyone else shouted out, "Booster!"

Ms. Boodle said, "Let's give Gordon a chance. Gordon, what do we wear on our feet in the snow?"

Everybody waited for Gordon to answer. Jason poked him. "That's easy!"

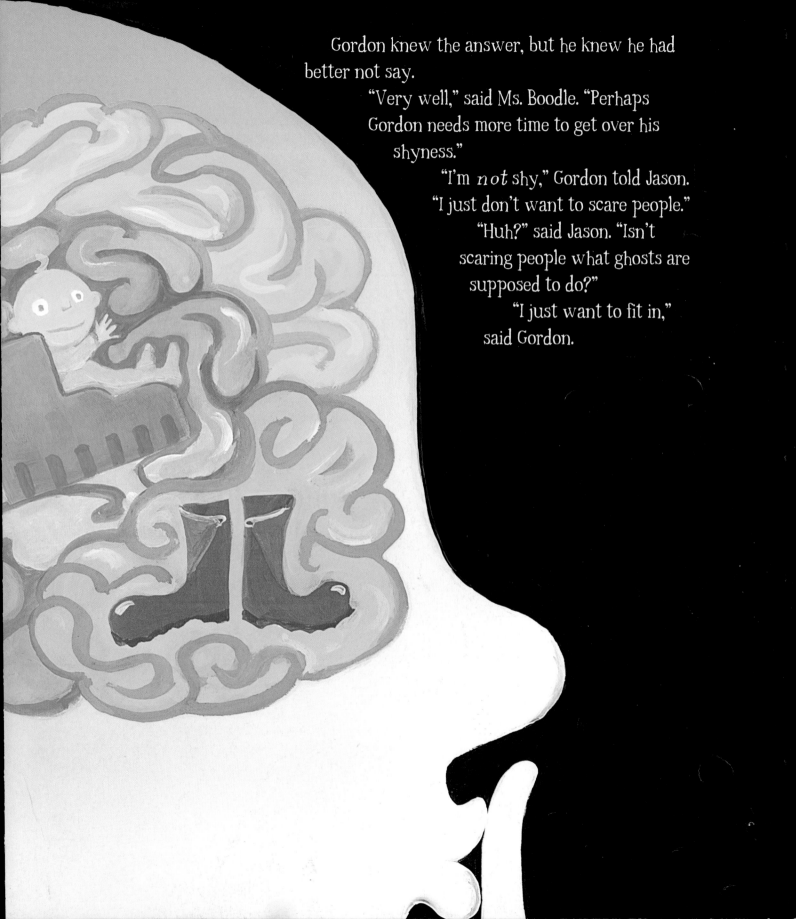

Gordon knew the answer, but he knew he had better not say.

"Very well," said Ms. Boodle. "Perhaps Gordon needs more time to get over his shyness."

"I'm *not* shy," Gordon told Jason. "I just don't want to scare people."

"Huh?" said Jason. "Isn't scaring people what ghosts are supposed to do?"

"I just want to fit in," said Gordon.

At lunchtime, Gordon couldn't wait to get to the cafeteria. That was the best place for making friends at school.

"What'd you bring in your lunch box?" asked Jason.

Gordon unfastened the latch. The lid lifted by itself. *CREEEEEAAK!*

Jason gasped. "Is that lunch box haunted or s-s-something?"

"Maybe," murmured Gordon.

Jason stood up and yelled, "HAUNTED LUNCH BOX! COME SEE!"
CR-R-REAK! went the lunch box.

The kids went berserk.

The cafeteria monitor turned out the lights to restore order.

AAAEEEEEEEIIIIIIOOOOOOOOOUUUUUUU! went the lunch box.

"Yikes!" yelled Jason. Like all the others, he ran screaming from the cafeteria.

"Bummer," muttered Gordon, alone in the dark. "I hate it when my mother puts surprises in my lunch box."

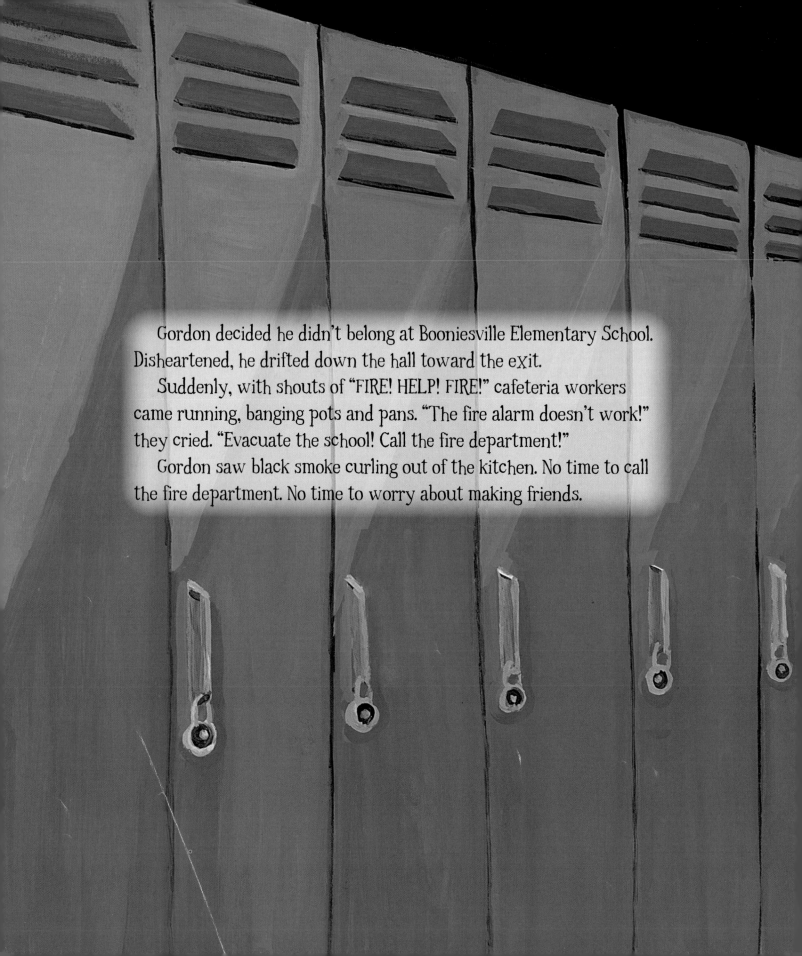

Gordon decided he didn't belong at Booniesville Elementary School. Disheartened, he drifted down the hall toward the exit.

Suddenly, with shouts of "FIRE! HELP! FIRE!" cafeteria workers came running, banging pots and pans. "The fire alarm doesn't work!" they cried. "Evacuate the school! Call the fire department!"

Gordon saw black smoke curling out of the kitchen. No time to call the fire department. No time to worry about making friends.

Far away in Ghost Town, students at Gordon's old school cocked their heads and smiled. "Sounds like our pal Gordon!" they said fondly.

And at the Booniesville fire station, firemen shouted, "Sounds like a big one!" They grabbed their gear and raced to their trucks.

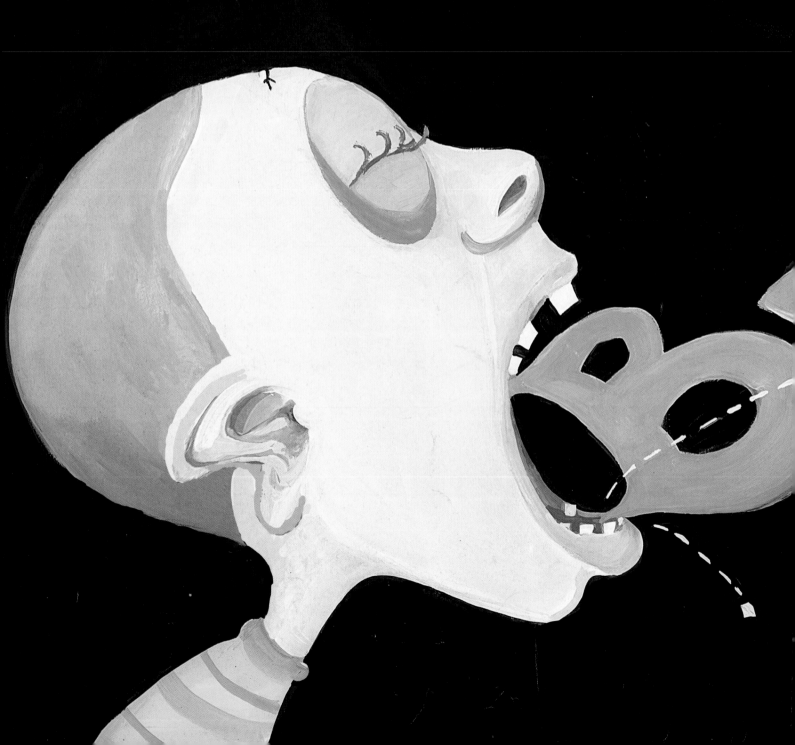

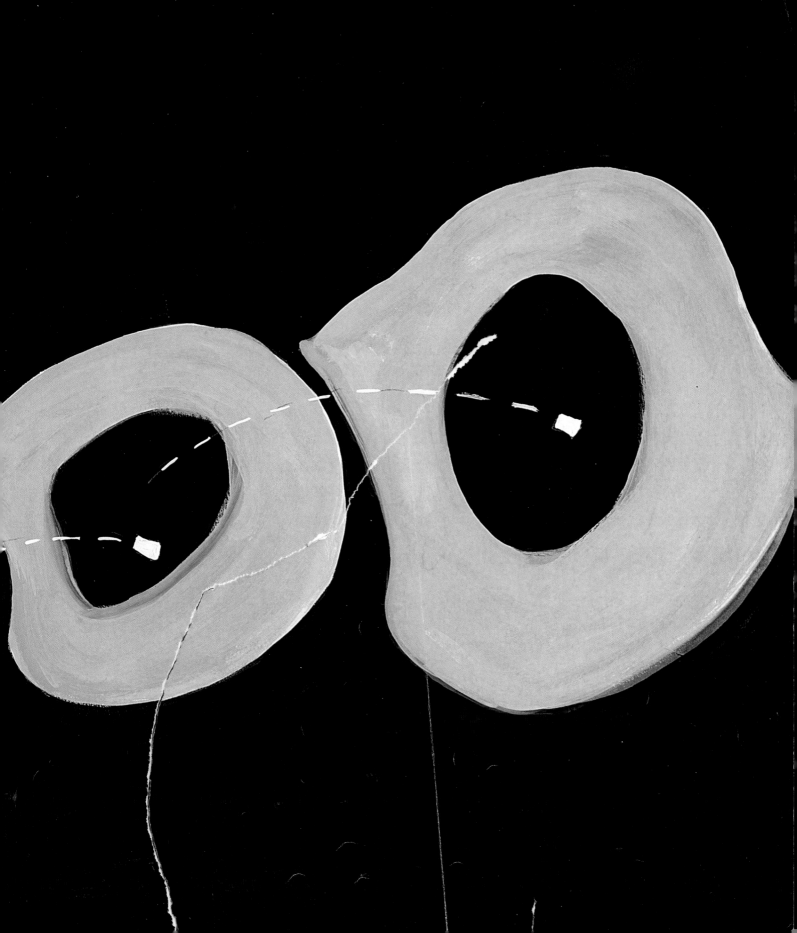

At Booniesville Elementary School, kids in every room blasted out of their seats. They remembered the rules for an emergency exit. Once outside, they still shook with fright. But they were safe.

Gordon flew to his house across the street. Watching out his window he could see everything. Fire trucks raced to the scene and doused the flames. The firefighters quickly confined the fire to the kitchen.

The next morning, Gordon didn't want to go back to that new school. He begged his parents to let him stay home.

"Not a ghost of a chance!" was their response.

When Gordon floated into his classroom, Ms. Boodle was writing his name on the board. *I'm probably in trouble about the haunted lunch box,* guessed Gordon. But then, "Hooray for Gordon!" his classmates were cheering!

When they had quieted down, Ms. Boodle said, "Gordon, your classmates have voted you Student of the Week. We're making a list of your most outstanding and endearing qualities."

Now everybody wanted to be friends with Gordon. He wondered if this was some kind of BOOby trap, but of course he didn't ask.

Scary
Hair-raising
Caring
Life-saving
Spooky
Modest
Quick-thinking

"Gordon," said Jason. "Sometimes it's fun to be scared, especially by a nice ghost like you."

Lisa said, "Gordon, could we have a Halloween party at your house?"

Gordon couldn't believe his ears. "A party at *my* house? That's a BOOOOO-tiful idea!"

"EEEEEEEEEEEEK! YIKES! AAAAAAAGH! COOOOOOOOOOOOOOOL!"